Lorgaire:

The Last Hunt

By Killian McCullin

Illustrated by Meghan McCullin

My brother drums the wheel of his blue 1969 Ford Mustang, making up for the lack of noise. The I-77 is just as quiet as our little visit to West Virginia. Even Lorgaire can have their car radios jacked, it seems. The window was costly enough to replace, so we didn't even bother with the radio. Plus, Cassius said he "enjoys the engine's roar," anyway.

"So I decrypted those messages dad sent. He says that there has only been one sighting and one disappearance. Our witness is Janet Mordecai, and our victim is Gerald Walsh. The witness posted her encounter to one of those blogs that dad runs. She said that while she was hiking up to her grandmother's house, she saw a wolf with black eyes staring her down. It disappeared as soon as it came. The victim was last seen by his girlfriend leaving their apartment. He was supposed to go for a quick hike, but he never returned." The drumming doesn't stop, and Cassius hasn't even looked over at me. "Did you get that?"

"Yeah, a wacko lady on one of dad's freak blogs said some wacko stuff, and a guy goes missing while hiking. I dunno, Donovan, seems like anything else that turns out to be a bust to me." He gives me a stern look and then looks back to the road.

"Hey man, if we get this finished fast enough, we can get back in time for Sibeal's birthday anyway. You know how dad is with this stuff. If this gets out there, it could flip the world on its head. It starts with a supernatural wolf, then it moves to ghosts, and next thing you know, vampires are celebrities, and werewolves raid towns and villages like it's the dark ages all over again." I try to tell him this in my most serious tone, but he still smirks.

"That is one slippery slope that dad got you to believe in." He avoids eye contact.

While he stares toward the road ahead, I look at him and say, "It could really happen. It's important to deal with this stuff as it comes up, not after the fact." Cassius doesn't even move his head; he just keeps one hand on the wheel and the other on the gear shift.

I shake my head and look back into my yellow notebook to piece together my thoughts and the files that dad sent.

* * *

Cassius and I ignore the small town of Black Mountain as we drive to Janet's grandmother's house, just on the edge of the nearby forest. I look over the badges and toss the one with Cassius' picture into his lap as we pull onto the gravel road.

"What kind of officers are we this time?" He eyes the road while glancing at the badge. "Wow, Federal Wildlife Officers, we haven't used these for a while. Why this time?"

"Yeah, well the idea is to convince her that this wolf she saw might have been a species that we had previously deemed extinct. Completely false, but hopefully, she will fall for it." I straighten my dark green tie and feel to see if my hair hasn't turned into a mess.

We park a reasonable distance from the white colonial-looking house with blue posts and more windows than necessary. Every single one has a curtain blocking it except that the kitchen seems open, and I see a figure moving around in there.

"So, this is the house?" Cassius asks, flipping down his mirror and fixing his collar and tie.

"Yep, Ms. Mordecai should be home. That might be her in the kitchen there; I can't quite tell." I say, failing to see any defining features of the figure.

"Well," Cassius says, opening his car door, "only one way to find out." I swing open my door and fall in behind him as we walk to the front porch.

Cassius rings the doorbell, and we go into our Federal Officer poses. He leans over to the window, fixing his short spiked hair. A face peeks through the curtains, vanishing just as quickly. Cassius attempts to look composed as the door opens.

An older woman greets us, wrinkles deep set in her dark skin. Her eyes have a bright blue shock for irises. "Hello, dears," Her voice creaks, yet she still sounds kind. "Oh, I thought you were my granddaughter. I guess she is yet to come home." I shake her hand as Cassius grabs out his badge.

"Hello, ma'am," Cassius lets the badge drop open and shakes her hand, "My name is Officer Sionis, and this is Officer Avaun." He gestures to me for the latter name, and I show my badge too. Dumb cover names, but I don't want to go through the effort of reprinting them. "We were wondering about something your granddaughter encountered recently. You said she isn't home?"

"Oh, no, she is out right now. Poor girl is always working." She sighs out of sympathy, but then she snaps back to her kindly demeanor as she looks at us. "Anyway, why don't you boys come in and have some tea?" She opens the door and gestures inside. We nod to each other and walk inside.

"So, you said you were Federal Wildlife Officers?" The older woman sips from her tea after holding a light conversation while making it. She sits in a rugged-looking chair with tight fabric cushions, the dark oak bookshelves lining the walls of this room look as though they are leaning, making the room feel packed.

Cassius nods, "Yes, and we are on a special field assignment. You see, the wolf that your granddaughter saw-"

"Old Black Eyes." She squints over her teacup, interrupting him.

"Sure. It could be an extinct wolf species, so we are trying to find some information about it. Given that it has a name, is it some local legend?" Cassius asks as he leans in, and I grab my notepad.

"Well, of course, deary. Old Black Eyes is an old spirit, as his name implies. He came here before the first colonists touched this land. He made his home in the Black Mountains, right up here, and the Cherokee knew to avoid him. The colonists didn't, and when they took the land from the Cherokee, they were never warned about Old Black Eyes. The colonists angered the spirit by building in his home, but luckily my ancestors came to protect this land and sprouted a Great Tree, which sealed away that dark spirit. Since then, everyone in my family has tended to the Great Tree. Until recently, when I got my hip replacement. I haven't been able to make the trek out there for a while. That must be why he's out here again."

Cassius looks at me with his classic "I don't know what any of this means" face before saying, "Uhm, thank you so much for your time. Got all of that, Avaun?"

"Yes, thank you again for your time, ma'am." I nod to him and wave my notepad.

The old woman stands slowly, "Oh dears, before you go," she slowly bends over next to her chair and brings out a rough green-dyed leather tome, "Take this if you would." She flips to a specific page written in ancient-looking Gaelic. "This here tells you how to tend to the tree. If you would be dears and do it for me?" She hands the book to me, and I nod. "Oh, this map here should help you find your way to the Great Tree." She gives me a slip of paper and holds my hand sweetly.

Before standing, Cassius takes a handful of small biscuits set out on a silver plate. The older woman smiles at him.

Cassius and I walk out, waving to her for the fifth time.

"Cassius," I lean over to him, "This is an old druid tome. Also, given how she talked about the spirit, it must be a Scarper."

He tosses a biscuit into his mouth, "That's one of those things that escaped Fomoria during the… uh, that one big war, right?"

I sigh, "Yeah, as if there weren't several. But yes, I think that this ritual in the book hasn't ever been completed. Usually, a Great Tree will completely banish a Scarper, so if it returns, that must mean that they are missing something from the ritual. I just need to find out what it is."

"Well," Cassius catches another biscuit, "Why don't we go to the tree. Who knows, we might find something interesting out there."

* * *

Dusk approaches rapidly, the enormous mountains assisting in that, and cool air rushes past us. I pause to look at the map the older woman had given us. "It's just up ahead, I think… yeah, here's the fork, so we take a left. Come on." Cassius follows behind as we twist through the unmarked trail. Winding between trees and bushes, I see clusters of red-capped mushrooms growing in frequency as we advance.

"There's our trail, I guess." Says Cassius, pointing his flashlight at the mushrooms. The afternoon threatens to turn to dusk at any moment.

I almost missed it at first, keeping my head down and looking for Mossweed. A towering tree as thick as a backyard shed stands high above the rest of the canopy. Redcap mushrooms surround it, and Mossweed clings to its trunk. "And there's our mark..." I say with quiet astonishment. "You seeing this, Cass?" I start circling the tree, slowly orbiting towards it.

"No, you're just high, Don, you ate that mushroom you saw earlier, and you have lost it ever since," Cassius says, half unaware. Nice to know he's just a jerk by nature.

"Sure. Anyway, all we need to do is restart the tree's healing process. It should be a pretty straightforward job this time." I smile over at Cassius, but it seems like my reassurance only reminds him that he isn't home. I clear my throat and continue, "Going off of my memory, all Great Trees are rapidly dying because they are not native to our world. So, a druid needs to be nearby to heal it and connect it back to the Otherworld temporarily, which will restart its time and revive it. This one looks like it's on its last leg." The bark is dry, unnaturally so, but underneath is a black tar-like substance pouring through cracks in some portions. The leaves at the top are an out-of-season brown and have tears.

"Because we aren't Druids, we need to start looking around for a couple of things." I snap to get Cassius to pay attention, as he is currently heavily engaged with studying the area. I hold the map and flashlight under my arm once he finally looks at me. "We need to look for any markings; they're going to look like some kind of rune, hard to miss, and we also need to find any bits of the ground where there are way too many insects. Those are druidic markings and should tell us something about healing the tree."

Cassius nods and starts sweeping the area with his flashlight, searching for any of those signs.

"Mmmh, I remember the smell of a Son of the Land well." A grumbling voice shakes the ground beneath me. I draw my silver dagger from the frog hanging on my belt and stand back to back with Cassius.

"You are Lorgaire," a hoarse chuckle orbits us quickly. "That is something I have not had the privilege of hunting for a long, long time." A dark shadow spins around us, going faster than I can track. "Oh, to hunt a hunter again. You were always the most enjoyable prey. Some of you were very clever, others strong, and others were just a pathetic excuse for a human. Quite frankly, all of you are, but it is interesting to see a show of strength, even if it is from an enemy clan. Your family has quite the reputation, Sons of the Land."

"Uhm, shadow thing, our family is the McLandon's, so you got that wrong," Cassius says, trying to ease the tension. Every time the shadow passes me, he shifts as though he will shove me out of this death circle we seem to be stuck in.

"Cassius, did you seriously not pay attention to dad's lore dumps at the dinner table? The ones about our family name and history? Whatever that isn't as important as getting out of here. We need to try again at a different time and come up with a plan." My breath is caught, and my words are short. We have dealt with some old things before, but nothing this old. It seems like, whatever this is, it fought in the *War of the Curse*. If it's that old, it's bound to be strong. "Look, Cassius, we did not come prepared enough for whatever this is. I knew we needed to take some time to plan and I should have said something. We need to leave, now!"

"Yeah, I am super well aware of how badly we need to leave, Don. If I took an awareness test right now, I'd ace it. That'd be a first." The shadow begins to orbit more slowly.

"What are you talking about?" I can tell he's nervous, but I need him to focus. "On three, we book it to opposite sides and meet up at the car. Do you remember the way?"

"Yeah, on three?" Cassius takes a deep breath.

"One…" The shadow slows even further.

"Two…" A streak of green forms in the shadow, trailing from its front.

"Three!" The shadow gets thicker and thicker. I hear squelching and cracking sounds as Cassius and I dart away. Trees whip past. Branches strike my face. Rocks threaten to roll my ankle as I dash recklessly down a creek. I practically throw myself up a gravel path. I hear four, no, eight footfalls behind me. Two ghastly snarls, and I see a flash of green from behind me fall on a tree ahead. A snap of jaws. Another snap. Something pierces my calf, and I trip, forcing the air out of my lungs. I feel nothing, thankfully. As I catch my breath, the adrenaline rushing through my body numbs the pain of pushing myself so hard and the wounds. A voice, discordant and torn, almost like a broken CD, calls out from both jaws behind me.

"The fate of your order was sealed long ago, Son of the Land. Run all you want, but the world will fall under our control. His-" the voices cut out, and for a second I hear fewer footfalls as I run into the last bit of light peeking through the trees and mountain tops, "Agh! You will fall, and all you know will fall with you. You run from fate itself. I have seen all of time; I have seen all that will be, and it ends with your blood, IT ALL-" the quick sound of hissing steam is all I hear as the voice cuts off from behind me. The light peeking through the trees saves me again.

I continue running through the light, bushy entrance to the thinner parts of the forest. The car is just up ahead. Cassius is to my left. We slam into the car, though he took more care with his landing. We both open the doors on either side and jump in. Cassius starts the car, and we are out of there. There is nothing but a cloud of dust, ruined suits, and dry mouths to show for our efforts.

***

Cassius helps me up the stairs, my leg still bloody from when the wolf bit me. Limping into the motel, I open my bag and pull out my medical kit. I take off my suit as carefully as possible and look at the wound. I can tell my calf is hurt badly, and I'll probably have a limp for the next couple of months. I pour alcohol on it, breathing heavily as it cleans out the multiple piercings. I lean in to see if there are any curse signs in or around the wounds, coming up with nothing. My fingernails don't show any sign of rotting, and none of my veins are discolored. Unable to remember any other signs of Damage Curses, I wrap up the wounds and hope that will be its extent.

I notice that Cassius still hasn't followed me in. I toss on some new clothes and stand up, limping out the door. "Cassius?" He's leaning over the railing, looking toward that forest, now covered in darkness. "Look, man, we can get it tomorrow. But for now, we need to rest and develop a plan."

Cassius turns his head and gestures with the hand holding his phone to his ear. He turns back, speaking to whoever is on the other side. "I don't want to be out here either. If I had it my way, I'd be back home yesterday. But Lorelai, these creatures threaten our daughter and us. This one could rip the world apart if we don't stop it. I just… bare with me, please. I'm trying to get back home as soon as possible, but this is another tough case."

All I can hear is a bunch of muffled, loud sounds coming from the phone. I turn back into the motel, but just before the door shuts behind me, Cassius says, "Okay, okay. I'll see what I can do."

More loud ringing, and then Cassius responds, yelling, "Money isn't infinite, yeah, I know that! As I said, I'm trying my damn best out here, but I can't just shoot everything I come across. I've tried that before. If it was that simple, I'd be out of a job."

Lorelai responds, and Cassius just sighs and talks back with an apologetic tone, "Yes, I know real jobs bring money back home. I'll try to work something out, but I can't just give this up. Donovan needs me. I mean, there's no way he'd survive without me here. Yeah, you got it… I love you." I let the door shut behind me as I grab some clothes to change into. Cassius comes in a minute after, rubbing his head, and plops onto the couch.

Before walking into the cramped bathroom, I turn to him. "Tomorrow, we're gonna head to the library and see what else we can find out. We're gonna get this thing."

* * *

Cassius and I sit in the local library, a pile of books between us. He sits on one of the five desktops typing, quickly looking, shaking his head, and repeating the cycle. I sit in the exact repetition, opening and skimming through one book before grabbing another. I have a couple of notes scribbled in my notepad, combining what I can find on the Cherokee and their stories about Old Black Eyes with the symbols and Gaelic text in the Druid tome. I skim the last book in my pile as Cassius sighs and leans back, rubbing his head.

"Yup, I got nothing," he reaches over and grabs my notepad, "What do you have?" Cassius reads over my small notes and leans forward, quickly gripping the mouse and typing on the keyboard. "Okay, maybe I was wrong. Come here for a second."

I get up and stand behind his chair, looking over his shoulder at the computer screen.

Cassius finishes typing and leans to the side. "Well, looks like the researcher has been beaten." He looks at me with a smirk and claps the notepad against the desk.

I take my notepad and jot down a couple more notes before moving back over and looking at the druid tome again.

Cassius throws his hands up. "What, I can't be right?"

"No," I tell him passively while reading from one of the books I closed before, "What you found isn't complete yet. Just give me a minute."

He spins in his chair as I type rapidly, looking between my new notes and the computer screen. I slap the table and look at him. "This, this is it! Look," I turn the computer screen towards him, scraping it across the desk, "I thought it was another one of those old stories that the Lorgaire used to cover up the truth, but I guess it was true. It's a clever cover-up. The truth was too unbelievable even for me, but what you were looking at gave me an idea. With some searching, I got the first account of Old Black Eyes, all the way over in Germany on the eastern frontlines of the War of the Curse."

Cassius leans into the screen and squints. "Mhm, I definitely see how this connects." He peeks around the screen and shakes his head.

I sigh and tilt the screen back over to me. "Okay, well, the story goes that there was a powerful Lorgaire named Jael Schiefer. He was a member of a shock troop, but he was a one-man army. He was so well known among the Fomorians at the time that they fled whenever he was on charge."

"Okay, so ultra-cool dude," He leans back, one arm over the back of his chair, "And that has what significance?"

"It is said," I look closely at the desktop screen in front of me, "He joined with the Emissaries of Equilibrium."

He doesn't even say anything, just tilts his head down and looks at me for an explanation.

"Man, you should try reading. Or paying attention when I talk. I've talked about them before. The Emissaries of Equilibrium was an alliance of old-world nations that believed the Otherworld was theirs to lay claim to. They aligned with the Fomorians in hopes that they could overthrow the ramshackle order after it fell. Anyway, Jael was part of this coalition, which was shockingly powerful, and he quickly became part of the Volk Circle: the governmental body."

"Dude," Cassius gestures with his hand behind him, "Why does this super ancient guy matter?"

"Just let me talk; I'm getting there." I shake my head as he groans, "Later, the Emissaries dissolved, and when they did, he joined with New Fomoria. Like many other Lorgaire who left the order, he was gifted a boon. They thought it would be ironic if he was given the ability to instill fear in the enemy, given that he once did it to them. So, there was a ritual performed on a Great Tree-”

“Hold on, I know this!” Cassius points at me, cutting me off, “We gotta reverse the ritual! Yes! I knew I had it in me to figure it out. You’re lucky to have me here, Don. Let’s go get ready to reverse engineer this curse thing.” He nods and stands, grabbing his jacket off his chair as he walks past me.

* * *

"Well, this feels familiar," Cassius says as we walk down the same path as before. "So, run the plan by me again if you could."

"Fine." Last time I do, who knows if he is listening or not. "So you will take this mixture," I hand him a cloth bag that is moist at the bottom, "and as soon as he comes by, you're going to take it with you running. If he gets too close, chuck it as far as you can and come back to the tree. I will have set up this warding circle that the Druid tome goes over by then. Simple, yeah?"

He nods, "Yeah." He sniffs the bag and then recoils, coughing and sneezing, "What is this stuff!?" He asks between fits.

"That is Mossweed, Other-vein–which is why it's red–and a sprinkling of salt to get it mixing. Those two things will draw him. He'll think you are a walking Gateway to Fomoria."

"Great, so he'll-" he sneezes again, "be chasing me double time to get back home? For a bunch of Fae that wanna destroy our home, Scarpers are pretty eager to get back to theirs."

We move past the Red Cap clusters and enter the small circular clearing around the Great Tree. I pull out my notebook and lay the tome against a large protruding root on the open page. With a handful of turnips from my bag, I walk in a slow orbit around the tree. I use my knife to carve a spiral rune into one and toss it hard into the ground next to me, chanting the old Gaelic I transcribed.

One turnip down. Two turnips. Tossing the third turnip brings another quadruple of thumps. I see Old Black Eyes, Jael, turning its shadowy face as it assesses its surroundings, having dropped from the air. I try to keep myself focused on the ward. Right now, I need to trust Cassius. I hear him whistle and then shout, "Hey, Mr. Schiefer! wanna go home?" Within an instant, I hear the paws clobbering the forest floor as Cassius books it into the trees.

With the fifth and final turnip tossed into the ground, the Mossweed near the tree gives off a dark green glow. The ward is up, which hopefully means that the wolf won't be snipping my hamstring while I do this. I kneel in front of the Druid tome, dropping as slowly as I can as to not upset my still fresh wound. I flip my yellow notebook to the correct page. The pages on the books move with the wind, but they don't threaten to flip on me. Before I can get the first word out, I hear Cassius breathing heavily, and then I hear a thud. Cassius is on his back just before a turnip. I reach out, and my hand smacks the air.

"Uh, Cassius, I think you're-"

"Don't tell me I am stuck out here," Cassius bangs on the invisible wall and sighs. "Look, you just focus on getting that tree fixed. I'll try and distract our friend."

As Cassius says that, I see the shadows coalesce into that form again, two pinpoint dots of green beaming into my soul, even when I don't look directly at it. I feel frozen in fear as the eyes pass over me and then onto Cassius. I drag in the air as though I hadn't inhaled for minutes. Shakily, I turn back to the pages and recite the first word of the spell.

"So, you like fear, huh? Or is that just a byproduct, not of your choice?" Cassius nearly shouts the words to get them out. I try to speed up without tripping over the aggressive, rough-sounding terms. I can't let that thing be the one that stops him from going back home.

"It's not fear. It's the acknowledgment that I am simply so powerful that you stand no chance against me. That freeze response you get is delightful. One sacrificing themselves for the pack. That's how it was when you Lorgaire hunted in packs. It is so odd that even though there are so many more of you Deantars, there are fewer and fewer Lorgaire. Soon, there won't be anyone to stop the return. I don't find the other Deantars as fun to hunt, though. They don't even know what I am. I feel that knowledge makes it all the more terrifying, doesn't it? Knowing what I am. You do know what I am, don't you? Cassius McLandon?" The wolf growls our last name.

"You know, I actually don't think I do. It's weird; I have hunted some *ugly* creatures in my time. Have you ever seen an Elf? Those things reek and nearly burn the eyes with how revolting they are. But you, man, I think you top the whole thing" the wolf chuckles at that one. Good, Cassius, use whatever you can to stall that thing. "Not one Fomorian I have ever seen has looked as ugly as you." There is a thud and Cassius grunts. He always takes it too far.

I take my time with these words, as these are longer and more difficult. One slip and I could ruin the whole spell and need to start over.

"You filthy Deantar! How dare you refer to me as though I am some common rank and file Fomorian! I was integral to the founding of the New Fomoria! I have killed hundreds of your ancestors, and I will kill many of your descendants!" There is a quieter thud, then it sounds like Cassius spits on the wolf. "Filth. You don't even know what I am capable of. Allow me to show you."

Complete silence. I hear nothing but my frantic recital of the complex druidic words. The ground around the tree begins to move slightly, green light rolling in through waves. It is the complete opposite of those neon green eyes the wolf has. It's natural, beautiful. The dark green light rolls up into the roots in waves, reaching higher and higher as I finish the final lines of the spell. As I chant the last words, I place my hand on the root that sticks out of the ground before me. It has a warm, cozy feeling that spreads up through the tree. The dark, cracked bark begins to heal, coming into a more natural brown, and the tar-like substance is sucked back within. In the final moments, I look to the seemingly unaware spirit sitting next to Cassius, looking down into his eyes. Cassius lays there catatonically, unmoving beside his breath. He doesn't even blink.

The wolf looks up at me and squints his eyes. It nods, and I hear it whisper right next to me, "I have killed him in a way worse than death." The dark green light builds up in the tree, and I watch as it blasts out and catches the wolf in a wave. It is stripped bit by bit, streaks of shadow flying away. It just sits there, staring at me. Those sickeningly bright green eyes burn into my mind, and I still see them there even though I know they aren't.

I run over to Cassius, falling down and grabbing his hand. "Hey, Cassius! C'mon, wake up!" I slap him lightly on his face. His head just rolls over. "Don't do this, don't do this to your wife, Sibeal, or me. Wake up!" I let out a desperate, ragged yell, looking around. I pick him up, holding him in my arms as I run back to the car. "I'm about to drive your car, man. Wake up!" He lays there catatonically. Under his eyelids, his eyes race as if he's in REM sleep. "Fine, your damn choice then." I toss him into the passenger seat and rifle through his pockets, finding the keys. I quickly jump into the driver's side and start the ignition. Not even the roar of the engine wakes him up. The wheels spin out as I rush to the motel.

* * *

I mix two handfuls of dry Mossweed, three slices of Spriteberry, and two vines of Red Cluster in my mortar and pestle. I quickly grind them into a paste before slapping it onto a wet rag and draping it over Cassius' forehead. His breathing has been consistent, which is lucky. I don't know what that wolf did to him, but it had to have been some sort of curse, and if this doesn't work, I'll have to move on to more narrow cures.

I grab a second towel and stand just as Cassius shoots up, holding the nearby coffee table and breathing heavily. "Sibeal!" He shouts, looking around. His posture drops, and he starts to look at his hands.

I walk over and drop the rag I'm holding. "Cassius, what is it? Do you feel something moving in your stomach? Maybe a pain in your palms?"

"What?" He looks at me, squinting his eyes, before sitting back and climbing onto the couch. "No, I wasn't cursed. Not like that, at least."

"What do you mean by that?" I ask him as I sit next to him on the very uncomfortable couch.

"It doesn't matter. I need to get back home." Cassius stands but loses his footing, falling back into the couch.

I put my hand on his shoulder, "If you don't want to talk about it, you don't have to. But you need to rest, so I'll just get packed up, and we'll see how you are later."

"I'm fine!" He shoves himself off the couch, walks over to his bag, and starts packing in loose clothes.

I shake my head and stand up, packing up my things. I can see Cassius angrily shoving clothes into his bag.

"I'm done with this, Don." He says, stopping and looking at me.

"Yeah, I know, Old Black Eyes isn't gonna bother Black Mountain ever again. I'm sure dad will find something later, but we've got a week of rest until then." I continue packing as I meet his eyes, but he continues looking at me. I stop as well.

"I mean with this. Being a Lorgaire. Once I go home, I'm not coming back." Cassius just stands there looking at me.

I try to see his eyes, checking for a mind curse. I didn't check for that, so that is possible. As I look, he leans forward.

"I'm not cursed, Donovan. I'm just done. This is too much, and it's not for me. Not anymore." He pauses before continuing to pack.

I walk over to him, "What do you mean? You're just done? We can't be done; there's always more monsters, always something hiding in the dark, Cassius! We have to go to it and destroy it. We're Lorgaire,

blood and trade."

"I never said anything about you quitting. You can keep hunting

for dad all you want, but I'm out." He keeps putting his stuff into his bag

nonchalantly.

"For dad?" I lean down and look into his eyes, "Who said that all

of this was for dad? This is for Sibeal, for the promise of a future."

He laughs, "Oh, this isn't what's best for Sibeal. What happens

when she's older? When does she start hunting with us? You think I

could put her life at risk for a possible victory?" He puts one last shirt in

his bag before looking back at me.

"We don't have to bring her into this." I say and take a step back,

keeping eye contact with him.

"And if we don't, it will be just the same as if I left right now. The

Lorgaire died long ago. We haven't been holding anything back. If the

world was going to cave in because of these monsters, it would have. It

will. And I want to be there for my daughter either way." Cassius zips the

large pocket of his bag, moving past me to grab his journal out of the

nightstand.

"Well, then we bring her into the fold, but we teach her carefully. She'll learn, and it will be fine." I gesture with my hands as if I were flattening the whole issue out.

"It won't be fine." He says passively, walking back over to his bag.

"Who told you that?" I step further back, over towards my bed.

"The wolf. He wasn't lying. He can see everything that's going to happen." He shoves his journal into his bag, his face becoming stern.

"Cassius, the Gifted Ones could only see certain things. They only could have seen major events, like the death of a clan-" Cassius quickly cuts me off.

"I saw Sibeal die!" He shouts and takes a couple of breaths.

"Cassius," I pause, thinking of how that could have been spun. There's no way… "It lied to you. I hadn't told you because I didn't think it was important. To scare the Lorgaire generals, Jael was given the ability to see into their consciousness and construct their worst nightmare in a way that benefitted the Fomorians. He just brought up a fear that you have."

"No, this wasn't fear, Donovan; this was the truth. I saw everything that would have happened if I had kept hunting. I saw my entire… her entire life. Right up until she cried out to me." He sits on his bed, facing away from me, toward the slatted blinds over the window. "I couldn't do anything. This thing that's coming, we can't kill it, and neither can she. All three of us tried, and we failed. I would rather live my life with my family while I can." He stands up, still facing the night sky. "I won't waste it fighting a battle we've already lost." He slings his duffle over his shoulder and walks toward the door.

"Cassius, you saw this thing; it all played out right before you. If it wasn't a lie, we can use that information against it!" I run up behind and grab his shoulder. He looks toward me. "We can fight. We may have failed in your vision, but now we know something, and we can make a plan."

"Donovan, there's no fighting fate. Like dad said," Cassius brushes my hand off his shoulder and opens the door, looking toward me, "A good hunter knows when they're prey." The door shuts behind Cassius. A minute later, I hear the roar of the Ford.

I sit down on the bed, sighing and rubbing my face. Pulling out my phone, I call the one number I never should. "Hey, dad. I know I shouldn't call, but there's a problem. I'm gonna need your help. I just found our biggest hunt yet."

Glossary

Deantar [DEEN-tar] - Fomorian word for human.

Druid [DROO-uhd] - A human particularly connected to the nature of Earth and the Otherworld.

Fey - Creatures native to the Otherworld.

Fomoria [fuh-MORE-ia] - A kingdom within the Otherworld.

Fomorian [fuh-MORE-ian] - A native of Fomoria.

Great Tree - Trees native to the Otherworld and were brought to Earth long ago. It must be tended to by a Druid, or it will slowly decay.

Gifted One - A human that was given supernatural abilities. Typically refers to those who allied with the Fomorians, but there were a few Lorgaire who were Gifted Ones.

Lorgaire [LAR-gair] - A human whose bloodline traces back to one of five orders of knights that initially formed an alliance with powerful Fey rulers against the Fomorians. Centuries have passed since the formation, and Lorgaire have fallen into myth, with many working in the shadows.

Otherworld - A world that exists alternatively to Earth. The home of all fey and supernatural beings. Its connection to Earth was sealed off centuries ago, but some creatures have managed to slip through.

Scarper - Refers to Fomorians that escaped the sealing off of Fomoria and subsequently the Otherworld.

War of the Curse, The - An ancient conflict between the forces of New Fomoria and the Lorgaire.